# Finch's First Flight

# FINCH'S FIRST FLIGHT

Story by STEVE CIABATTONI
Illustrations by ANNIE WILKINSON

ISBN: 9798375968131

To Janet, who lifts me off the ground.

Special thanks to Duncan Ewald for his encouragement and guidance, to Paul Sarkis for the title, and to a little bird at LaGuardia Airport who gave me the idea.

This is the story of a little bird named Finch
who lived at the airport.

A bird who lived at the airport?

Was this bird a pilot?
An explorer?
A world traveler?

No. Finch was none of these things.

In fact, Finch was afraid to fly.

Instead of flying, Finch hopped around the airport eating popcorn or whatever else messy travelers left behind.

One day, Finch hopped near a small boy eating a giant pretzel. Finch waited for a piece to fall, but the boy never dropped a crumb.

Instead, he looked at Finch and said, "Hello, little bird!"

"Hello," Finch said.

"Are you at the airport to teach the pilots how to fly?" the boy asked. "I bet you are because birds are so good at flying."

"Uh... Yes, that's right. I am an expert flyer," Finch said. He didn't want to admit that he was afraid to fly.

"I'm nervous about flying today," the boy said. "It's my first time. Would you help me be brave like a pilot?" he asked Finch. "I'll give you some of my pretzel if you do."

Finch loved this idea. He'd get a free pretzel, and he wouldn't really have to fly himself.

"Sure! I'll help you," Finch said to the boy.

Just then, the boy's parents told him it was time to fly. He stuffed Finch into his jacket pocket and boarded the plane.

After the boy buckled himself into a window seat, he whispered to Finch, "Thanks, little bird. I'm so glad you're with me. I'm not as scared now that I have such an expert flyer for a friend."

"N-n-no p-p-problem," Finch said, shaking as the engines rumbled and every seat jiggled. The plane roared down the runway and then nosed up toward the sky.

Finch was too scared to look and hid deep inside the boy's pocket.

Up in the bright blue sky with its soft white clouds, the boy was amazed at what he saw. Below him were silver roads and blue rivers that curled around bridges, baseball fields, and green and golden farms.

"I don't know why I was so afraid to fly," the boy said. "It's beautiful up here."

"Little bird, what's your favorite thing to look at when you fly?" the boy asked Finch.

"Little bird?" the boy asked again.

Again, Finch didn't answer. Finch was so frightened and so deep inside the boy's pocket that he couldn't hear a thing.

"Hey, little bird!" the boy said, tapping his pocket. "Are you sleeping? Why are your eyes closed?"

"Oh," Finch said. "I was... just thinking about landing. You know, pilot stuff."

"Look at what you're missing," the boy said.

Finch was scared, but now he was also curious.

Slowly, he inched out from the boy's pocket, pressed his beak against the window and saw everything – the sun up above and all the trees and tiny little towns below.

Finch's eyes grew wide as the plane floated through a puffy white cloud. Then he saw big snowy mountains and a clear blue lake that was as shiny as a mirror!

"Wow!" Finch said.

Maybe flying isn't so scary, Finch thought.

Maybe... he could even try it himself?

Finch started to flap his wings – slowy at first, then as fast as he could. He hovered for a bit and soon was taking his very first flight up and down the aisle of the airplane.

Every passenger shouted and pointed at Finch. They swung their neck pillows, magazines, headphones, eye masks – anything to stop Finch from flying.

Since Finch was new to flying, he didn't fly in a straight line, making him harder to catch.

Passengers ducked as Finch swooped down, then up, then left, then right.

Finch went "Tweet, tweet!" as a flight attendant fell backwards, knocking over all the chips and cups and bottles and cans on the snack cart.

"Be careful, little bird!" the boy shouted as he grabbed his pretzel and raised it over his head – hoping to lure Finch back to his seat.

Finch saw the pretzel and zipped back down the aisle to have a nibble after his wild ride. Finally, everyone calmed down as the pilot came out of the cockpit.

"Thank you for catching that bird," the pilot said to the boy. "You're very brave, but you know birds aren't allowed on planes."

"Yes, but he's a special pilot-training bird," the boy explained. "He was just on the plane to help me because I was afraid to fly."

"Oh," said the pilot. "Then I better take him to the cockpit so he can help us land. Ok?"

"Yes," said the boy. "I'm a pretty good flyer now, so I don't need the bird's help anymore."

The pilot scooped up Finch and took the tired, pretzel-filled bird up to the cockpit.

Finch sat on the captain's hat for the rest of the flight and watched as the plane came down through the clouds and landed safely.

As the boy left the plane, he waved to the pilot and to Finch. "Thank you for helping me to fly, little bird," he said.

"Same to you," said Finch flying past the boy and into the airport. But Finch didn't stop there.

Finch flew out of the airport and then up and up, high into the sky.

"I like it up here," Finch said. "I don't think I'll ever come down."

The end.

Made in the USA
Middletown, DE
26 February 2023